JANE YOLE

# How Do Dinosaurs Choose Their PETS?

Illustrated by

# MARK TEAGUE

SCHOLASTIC INC.

This book was originally published in hardcover by The Blue Sky Press in 2017.

ISBN 978-1-338-28093-7

Text copyright © 2017 by Jane Yolen. Illustrations copyright © 2017 by Mark Teague. All rights reserved.
Published by Scholastic Inc., *Publishers since 1920.* SCHOLASTIC and associated logos are trademarks
and/or registered trademarks of Scholastic Inc.

12 11 10 9 8 7 6 5 4 3 2 1                    18 19 20 21 22 23

Printed in the U.S.A.                          40

First Scholastic paperback printing, February 2018

Book design by Kathleen Westray

A special book for Sam—J. Y.

For Laura—M. T.

How does a dinosaur
pick out his pet?
Does he go on the prowl
with a stick and a net?

Does he head to the zoo
and take home a big cat?
(And what does his mom
have to say about that?)

Does she drag a huge elephant
back in a wagon
with both its long trunk
and its wee tail
a-dragging?

Or, speaking of dragons,

does she go acquire

a high-flying beastie
who loves to
breathe fire?

Does he pick out
a boa constrictor for play?
Does it look at his dog
in a very odd way?

AMPELOSAURUS

Does he sneak an iguana

inside of a cap?

Or lead home a kangaroo
by a long strap?

Does he ask for a manatee,

maybe a whale,

or wish for a shark

he can keep in a pail?

Does she carry off tortoises,

zebras, a mink?

Giving them hay

and a cola to drink?

Is that what you think?

No . . . a dinosaur doesn't.
She knows what to do,
and she never brings anything
home from the zoo.

DO NOT
FEED

He goes to a shelter

or pet store

or farm

to find a small creature

who will do no harm.

He brings home a kitten

or hamster or pup

that he can teach manners

as they both grow up.

She cares for her pet,
and gives love

even more.

Big hugs to your friend,
little dinosaur.